Bank Street

ABOUT THE BANK STREET READY-TO-READ SERIES

More than seventy-five years of educational research, innovative teaching, and quality publishing have earned The Bank Street College of Education its reputation as America's most trusted name in early childhood education.

Because no two children are exactly alike in their development, the Bank Street Ready-to-Read series is written on three levels to accommodate the individual stages of reading readiness of children ages three through eight.

Level 1: GETTING READY TO READ (Pre-K–Grade 1)
Level 1 books are perfect for reading aloud with children who are getting ready to read or just starting to read words or phrases. These books feature large type, repetition, and simple sentences.

Level 2: READING TOGETHER (Grades 1–3)
These books have slightly smaller type and longer sentences. They are ideal for children beginning to read by themselves who may need help.

Level 3: I CAN READ IT MYSELF (Grades 2–3)
These stories are just right for children who can read independently. They offer more complex and challenging stories and sentences.

All three levels of The Bank Street Ready-to-Read books make easy to select the books most appropriate for your child's development and enable him or her to grow with the series step by step. The levels purposely overlap to reinforce skills and further encourage reading.

We feel that making reading fun is the single most important thing anyone can do to help children become good readers. We hope you will become part of Bank Street's long tradition of learning through sharing.

The Bank Street College of Education

P9-CCM-990

ANNIE'S PET

A Bantam Book/July 1989

*Published by Bantam Doubleday Dell Books
for Young Readers, a division of Bantam
Doubleday Dell Publishing Group, Inc.
1540 Broadway, New York, New York 10036.*

Associate Editor: Randall Reich

*Special thanks to James A. Levine, Betsy Gould,
Erin B. Gathrid, and Herb Valen.*

Library of Congress Cataloging-in-Publication Data

*Brenner, Barbara.
Annie's pet.*

*(Bank Street ready-to-read)
"A Byron Preiss book."
Summary: On her way to the pet shop to buy an animal with her
birthday money, Annie buys a toy, a collar, a dish, and a
leash and discovers that she has no money left for a pet.
[1. Pets—Fiction] I. Ziegler, Jack, ill.
II. Title. III. Series.
PZ7.B7518An 1989 [E] 88-7965
ISBN 0-553-05833-9
ISBN 0-553-34693-8 (pbk.)*

Published simultaneously in the United States and Canada

PRINTED IN THE UNITED STATES OF AMERICA

Bank Street Ready-to-Read™

Annie's Pet

by Barbara Brenner
Illustrated by Jack Ziegler

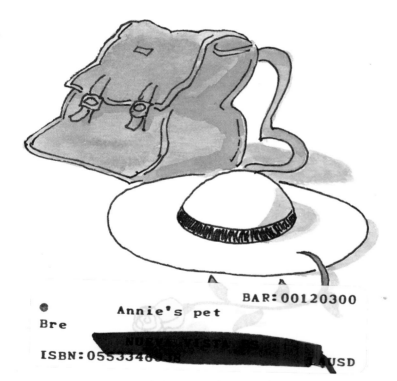

A Byron Preiss Book

BANTAM BOOKS
NEW YORK · TORONTO · LONDON · SYDNEY · AUCKLAND

On her birthday, Annie went to the zoo. That's where she got a great idea.

"I have five birthday dollars," she said to her family. "I'm going to buy an animal."

Annie didn't know
what kind of animal she wanted.
But she knew
what kind she didn't want.

"I don't want a bear," she said.
"Bears are too hairy."

"I don't want a snake.
You can't take a snake for a walk."

"Try not to buy too big an animal," said her father.

"You don't want too small an animal," said her mother.

"Get a wild animal," said her brother.
"I don't want a wild animal," said Ann.
"I want a *pet*."

The next day, Annie put on her hat and her backpack.
"So long, everybody," she said.
"I'm going to buy my pet."

Annie walked down the street
until she came to a house.
There was a girl with a bird
in front of the house.

The bird gave Annie an idea.

Annie called to the girl,
"Will you sell that bird
for five dollars?"
"Not for a million dollars.
I love this bird."

"But I need a pet to love, too,"
said Annie.
"Try the pet store," said the girl.
And she went inside with her bird.

Annie walked a little more.
She came to a toy store.
The store gave her an idea.

"Do you have toys for pets?"
she asked the man inside.
"All kinds," said the man.
"Swings, rings, bells, balls."

"I'll take a ball."
"That will be one dollar,"
said the man.
Annie gave the man one dollar.
She still had four dollars.

Annie walked a little more.
She came to a gift shop.
A pretty tan cat was sitting
in the window.

Annie went into the shop.
"How much is that cat in the window
she asked the woman.
"That cat is not for sale,"
said the woman.
"We do not sell pets.
But we do sell pet collars."

Now that's a great idea," said Annie.
A collar—not too big, not too small."

Annie bought a collar for one dollar.
She still had three dollars.

Annie walked a little more.
She went into a store
in a shopping mall.
She saw a nice red pet dish
and a nice red pet leash.
They each cost one dollar.
Annie bought the dish and the leas

"Now I have all the things
I'll need for my pet," she said.

Annie's long walk had
made her very hungry.
So she stopped to buy a little snack.
It only cost one dollar.

t last, Annie came to the pet store.
ie looked in the window.
here were pets of every size and kind.

This is it, " cried Annie.
This is where I'll buy my pet. "

Annie reached into the backpack
to get her money.
But the money was gone!

She thought about what
she had spent—
one dollar for a toy . . .
one dollar for a collar . . .
one dollar for a dish . . .
one dollar for a leash . . .
and one dollar for a double-dip cone!
Five—Annie had spent
all five birthday dollars!

Annie sat down on a stone step
to have a good cry.
But then she looked up
and saw a sign that read:

That's when Annie got
the greatest idea of all!
She jumped up and ran inside.

"I'm looking for a pet," said Anni
"Can you give a pet a good home?"
asked the woman behind the desk.
"Yes," said Annie.
"I have a collar, a toy, a dish,
and a leash for my pet.
But I don't have any money."

"o you have love?" asked the woman.

"n, yes, I have a lot of that, " said Annie.

"hen I have just the pet for you, "

woman said.

And she did.